THE LIGHTNING AND THE SNOW:
Seven Stories For the Inner Child

Alexander De Witte

DORMOUSE PUBLICATIONS

1

THE LIGHTNING AND THE SNOW
Seven Stories For the Inner Child

Copyright 2019 Alexander De Witte

All Rights Reserved

Cover Designer: *Karen Lennox Williams*: **kazziedesigns@yahoo.com**

Cover image: Joanne Price

Contents

In Memory Of

Margareta Alphonsina Alberta
De Witte
(my mother and my friend)

Foreword

It has always been that children's stories capture the imagination – and for obvious reasons. Who does not appreciate how a child can be lit up by stories? And yet, in my world, there exists a child within each of us, who can still reach for the light of long lost innocence. Yet the adult has travelled paths that the child has not. And this adds an element of nostalgia. It also gives us the opportunity to weigh just what we have lost, what we *should* have lost and what might have been *better retained*.

Allowing adults the space to access old memories of what formed them as children, opens up a dimension that is not quite the playground of children's story. But it *is* a storied space nonetheless – one which prefigures possibilities of personal 'redemption' by making peace with the dramas of the past and retrieving, plus recycling, all the things from our lost innocence that would serve us well today. Cynicism does not serve us well. Recapturing the magic, on the other hand, through shared memories of what was both wrong *and* right – evoked by stories we can all relate to – seems to me a highly worthwhile and potentially useful form of nostalgia and a vehicle into fresh joy – as we transmute what might have trapped us into something which allows the burdened soul to fly once more.

I offer these stories to all adults as a way of accessing some of those spaces that might otherwise prove to be nigh impossible to reconstruct. Revivifying ancient memories we can all relate to, offers the prospect of bringing us together to transcend the baggage which may have blighted our life force and weighed us down intolerably.

I chose seven stories for a reason. Seven is the number of knowledge and erudition. The cover of the book was snapped, in fact, by my old classmate at school, Joanne Price (nee Openshaw) at summer solstice 2019. When I saw it, there was instant recognition of how it showed the inner light, seeking to prevail in the face of all the surrounding darkness.

The nostalgia of old school days is one universal motif that our social media contact lists attest strongly to. We long to be connected to those things which shaped us. Even when they disappoint in some ways and seem shrouded in darkness, elements of our shared stories nevertheless offer us a unique sort of light. Those stories good *and* bad still constitute us. We can move beyond the not-so-good and still celebrate all the beautiful memories that never depart.

In this short collection there are two, one hundred word micro-stories, and five longer ones. There are mythologies and fantasies, other worlds that we travel to and other worlds which break into this scene of time. The one common thread is that all these stories seek to evoke nostalgia. That can be a messy and unproductive space. But it can also allow us to recollect fondly, with a smile on our face. If this is achieved in this short collection then it will have done its job.

Maybe you cannot change the past. But you can certainly start a new adventure, wherein you take the best elements of those old narratives and weave them into something more aligned with who you wish to be, right now.

Best Wishes on that journey.

Alexander

28th June 2019

Chapter 1

Such Things That Follow You.

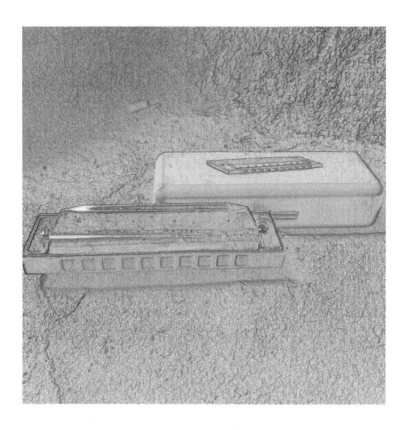

14

"Let's find a way to get in," Pavel said.

They were horsing around on Halloween eve.
Tomorrow would be the *really* scary day. So a night
time adventure sneaking into the old abbey, offered
the prospect that a very entertaining time might be
had... with not quite so much fear in the air. Neither
boy had returned home after school. Both were still in
uniform.

"How are we going to do that? I'm not sure that a site
such as this will have been left unsecured" Peter
replied.

There had been stories about this place. You know,
the type of lore that the older youths passed around
to see who had the most nerve in being the 'keeper of
the dark secrets'. This was always the stuff of urban
legend, relating to mysterious places in your locale. It
made the stories so much more real when they were
about places you knew, rather than those timeless
tales devoid of geography and with mere smatterings
of history. Everyone, of course, aspired to be the cool
kid who knew the stuff that nobody else did.

"Let's go round the back and try the door to that old
chapel. Sam said there is a phantom who unlocks the
door if he knows that someone of interest has
intentions to visit. He reckons this ghost knows your

deepest secrets. Apparently he is supposed to be an old monk from the 1830s – one of the first in holy orders to play the recently invented harmonica."

"Get away with you, Pavel. You've got rocks for brains."

The two boys walked around the side of the abbey and climbed a wall. They dropped down around eight feet on the other side into a somewhat dishevelled, old garden area. They were supple though, so it did not jar their bones. Walking up to the solid oak door of the chapel's entrance, Pavel turned the ring-shaped black metal handle and pushed against it. It was hefty but the door was unlocked and the boys were able to enter.

"See," Pavel said with a bold tone and grin, "he knew we were coming!"

"Shut up lad!" the retort flew back.

Luckily they had prepared by bringing powerful torches, because it was pitch black. As the chunky door once more filled the frame with a clunk, both boys felt the hairs on the back of their neck stand to attention, like warriors ready for battle.

"Are you feeling that Peter?"

"Yes, yes I am."

Swinging their search light beams around to get some orientation they could make out that they were in a very large old hall with a number of pews and a raised altar near the west wing of this sizeable room.

Pavel had appointed himself leader of this expedition without asking and so he set off in the direction of a door he could recognise the outline of, which seemed to be around forty feet away. Peter, looking around and swinging his beam continually left then right as they went, was not sure this was such a good idea. Then, just as Pavel placed his hand on the door knob of this new room that was calling for exploration, the silence was pierced. It was the sound of a harmonica. It began playing out an other-worldly melody. 'No time to lose,' both boys thought simultaneously. Without a word they dashed back to the entrance, opened the heavy door and scaled the wall they had dropped from just a few minutes earlier and fled.

Five minutes later, they both stopped and stooped, hands on knees, panting for breath.

"Never again and we will not speak of it," Peter said.

"Why not?" Pavel countered.

"Because this kind of thing has a way of escalating, that's why! It never happened, Pavs."

"Are we going to meet up tomorrow still? We have got to get out and knock on some doors, Pete."

"Anything will be better than this, lad" the still shaken Peter responded. "Let's meet at eight at Polly's like we talked about the other day."

"Right you are, see you then."

Both boys headed home. It was nearly 11.30pm when Peter attempted his usual *sneaking into the house unnoticed* routine. Unfortunately for him, his father was waiting up.

"What time do you call this?"

"Bedtime?" Peter tried to make light of his father's inquiry.

"I'm not laughing son. You have school tomorrow. If you do not curb your irresponsibility then you will be grounded. Don't push it any more than you have my boy."

"Yes, dad." Truth was, Peter did not care about the future, only being able to enjoy himself on

Halloween. So he placated his father with faux humility, as he often did. Of course it worked a treat as usual. You had to be smart these days in order to wrap your parents around your little finger. And Peter *was* smart.

"Anyhow son, before you go to bed. I know you've not been home since finishing school. Something came for you in the post today."

The man handed his son a small package. It was addressed to him and written in a calligraphy style of writing. The boy looked at the packaging and the writing, wondering who might have sent him this. He was certainly not expecting any delivery.

"Well, are you going to open it, or not?"

"Tomorrow perhaps, dad. I need to sleep."

The boy went to the kitchen, poured himself a tall glass of iced milk and retired to his room. Upon entering it he set the package down on his desk and switched on his table lamp. It shone down on the rectangular box in an inviting way. "I'll open this tomorrow" he said out loud, before climbing into bed and dropping off in no time at all.
The night seemed to go on forever. It was a restless one. There were dreams aplenty. There was a

moment, after waking from slumber, that the pull cord when yanked, failed to switch on the bedroom light. Yet this waking was also a dream, one that felt all too vivid. And when that light failed to come to the rescue... it started... the slow melodic tune. It was emanating from *somewhere* in the room. It seemed familiar somehow. Next thing Peter knew he was hearing the sound of a magpie while still in the twilight of returning consciousness, after his repose. 'What a strange dream sequence' he thought. But he could remember only fragments of it.

After a satisfying stretch and a coming-to yawn, he sat upright on the bed and cleared his eyes by gently massaging his eyelids with his fingers, as you sometimes do in your waking-up ritual. And then he saw the package. 'Must open it' he thought. And so he did. Inside the box he found no note of any kind, no explanation, no receipt or return address; not even a 'thank you for your custom' note, accompanying his new harmonica.

"Shit." He said.

The school day flew by. There had been a buzz of anticipation already prefiguring the atmosphere which would descend later for those venturing out, each with their very own jack o'lantern. But the buzz was really about entertainment. The ancient idea of

Samhain had been buried by modern rituals. The old ways, which celebrated the thinning of the veil between the worlds, was hardly in evidence. After their experience in the abbey the previous night however, Peter was not sure that the veil needed to be any thinner. At least he, Pavel, Polly and Sam would be hanging out, granting safety in numbers. He was still unsettled by recent occurrences. The evening itself passed quite uneventfully, during their visits to homes around their neighbourhood. Still, on three separate occasions, Peter believed he had seen a hooded figure watching from behind a tree, wearing what resembled a monk's garb. He swore he must be imagining this, because nobody else said a thing; not even Pavel, who had shared the previous night's experience. They were soon to go their separate ways, when approaching the final house they would visit, they passed close by a large yew tree. Peter felt the hairs on his neck stand up. He saw a little bit of a cloak just four feet to his right protruding and clinging to a human shape and then a voice in a hoarse and slow, loud whisper "Play my harmonica."

The others were completely oblivious, while Peter felt he was going crazy. What *was* this thing on his tail? The four companions parted company and made their way to their respective homes at a quarter to midnight. It was Friday, so no school the next day. As Peter got home his mother asked "nice time, love?"

But Peter was in a world of his own. He went straight to his room and retrieved the harmonica from its case. He lifted it to his lips. He was about to play his first note. Then he thought. 'No, what would I be summoning?" And so, he placed the instrument down on his bedside table.

Peter went to sleep hoping that the morning would come quickly and this whole Halloween thing and the monk's appearances would cease. 'All Saints Day should clear all that mucky energy out', he thought. When he awoke at 2.30am he could feel something in the room. It was watching. He could feel it. He did not move. He even held his breath. This thing, whatever it was, was moving. Peter pulled the duvet fully over his head. He courageously peeked out after three minutes or so, looking to his right. And there he could see an old toy of his, a foam-stuffed rabbit, wearing a waistcoat and hat with a nefarious grin on its face. It was glowing, as if lit up like a lamp. The rabbit carried many associations for Peter. It had been there when all the terrible things had happened. It was a witness to things that should not ever be seen. He was petrified. He pulled the duvet tightly back over his head. Then he heard the beginnings of an ominous rumble. It sounded like steps bounding menacingly up the stairs, homing in, as if some *thing*, some marauder, were about to fling open his door and kidnap him. And then the voice entered his head, much more forcefully than earlier, near the tree. This was a demand, a bellowing: "PLAY MY HARMONICA."

Sweating and in a panic, Peter reached for the harmonica. He felt something icy grab his hand. Quickly withdrawing it back under the duvet, he pressed the mouth organ to his lips, barely able to breathe. But then he managed a note. Next came a tune and finally the refrain, just like the one he had heard in the abbey – which was strange, because Peter *could not play harmonica.* But... the other things had stopped and Peter now felt calm. Lifting the duvet from over him he looked into his room. There, sat on his chair, by the desk, was the hooded monk.

"Are you the monk I heard in the abbey?"

"Yes, I knew you were coming and so I unlocked the door. I also sent you the harmonica – just like the one I used to play in the 1830s and 1840s."

"Why did you follow me?"

"I was an exorcist, Peter. I used music in order to overcome the presence of evil afflictions and so that a person might become calm. I knew that your past had been haunting you and that these things would come to try and take you away through the veil and into the realms of madness and affliction, this Halloween. They are tormentors."

"So why did you come *to me*?"

"All that you have been through is for a reason. These things have shaped your soul. If you had succumbed to the darkness, you would have been capable of great evil. Other young men have been in your place and slid into darkness. But you are now to be the master of the harmonica. It will be your job to teach people the power of music to soothe the spirit and liberate the soul."

"What else must I know?"

"When you saw me you were fearful. You imagined that all the tales about me meant that I was from the darkness. People make their own fears into demons. They put the darkness out into the shadows, so that they can believe it is not inside them. You must show them not to judge by appearances and by your music you will enchant their souls, in order to bypass the stubbornness of their minds. All my tunes are now within you. Go. Be free and show all those who are lost, the narrow pathway through the shadows."

And then the monk was gone. It was All Saints Day now. In a few hours the Sun would rise on a new chapter. Peter slept soundly for the rest of the night. His new harmonica safely clasped in his hand.

Chapter 2

The Octopus and the Wheel

Two seagulls glided serenely over the sea, around a quarter of a mile from the coast of Dover and in parallel to the shore. In almost perfect unity they skimmed inches above the calm surface. One bird seemed to crane its neck slightly toward the other, as if preparing for conversation. Its companion said "Something I've always been curious about, Fred."

"And what's that, Florence?"

"We've flown many a mile and yet I've always wondered, why does the sea move?"

"Oh that's easy," came the reply. "We have been studying that on my BSc in Geology and Oceanography at the University of Brighton."

"You never told me you were studying. Do tell."

"Well," elaborated Fred "the moon exerts gravitational pull on Earth..."

"What?" interrupted Florence. "That light in the sky, by which we sometimes enjoy a leisurely evening tryst?"

"Yes, but it is more than that! You see, the Sun's warmth and air current shifts, as well as the rotation of Earth, bring about waves."

29

"Oh Fred, you can be *such* a bore!"

"Well, you DID ask!"

"Honestly Fred, I was talking with some of the girls about how strange it all is – you know when I was at the salon the other day having my claws and beak done. Anyhow, Ethel said an ancient American Bald Eagle with great eyesight, a truly wise bird, had told her husband Cecil the Cormorant on one of those fancy retreats they do these days, that there is a strange creature at the seabed, goes by the name of Octopus, who turns a huge wheel. Apparently, Octopus is very knowledgeable and understands just how to make everything balance out. He cannot always protect every ship though and disasters do still sometimes happen."

"Get away with you! This is the twenty first century."

"Well look, not every newfangled idea is great or correct just because it is modern. I'm with the story of Octopus. Makes sense to me."

"That's as may be but how would you expect me to continue on a university degree if I believed codswallop like that!"

"I say we call upon capable help to referee this dispute and maybe test this theory, Fred."

"Deal" came the reply.

And with that Florence raised three shrill and piercing "caws", which carried over the surface of the waters and toward the nearby White Cliffs. Around three minutes later, a guillemot arrived on the scene. "What can I do you for, Florence?"

"Hello George, long time no see! Fred and myself have two differing theories about why the sea is always moving. He thinks it is all explained by science and I got a different account relayed to me, about Octopus, who lives under the sea and who turns a wheel left and right, which moves the water around."

"Ah, I see. Are you saying you would like me to take a look for you?"

"Those were exactly my thoughts when I called out to you."

Without any further prompting, George set off soaring high into the sky. He almost disappeared from sight. The next thing Florence and Fred knew, a streak of high speed guillemot had shot like a bullet from a gun, past them and into the water. George was streamlined of shape and within around forty seconds the momentum of his dive had propelled him right to the seabed. As he looked around, he saw some thick vegetation and it looked as though there was something else. He made his way closer to the greenery to see what this was.

Meanwhile, at the surface, there was not a little agitation as bubble after bubble rippled its way up and popped at the surface.

"Do you think he'll be okay down there, Fred?"

Fred shrugged his shoulders, like only Fred could.

Down below, George could see a large, strange-looking creature, with eight arms all moving around wildly. These arms were doing the job of turning what looked like a huge ship's wheel. George was flabbergasted. He was about to turn round and return to the surface with the verdict, when he heard a loud booming voice – "You there Guillemot, what are you doing?"

George told Octopus all about the challenge he had been given then said, "Please, it is time for me to return, to tell Florence and Fred what I discovered."

"What?" Octopus replied. "You certainly shall not tell them that you found me here."

"Why should I not report back my findings? The truth is important in resolving all manner of disputes."

"Do you know what problems that would cause? Have you never heard of the Paparazzi? Were they all to come to know that I am here, it would never be possible again to find even a moment's peace. All that flashing photography and the constant demands for interviews."

"Oh I see," George replied, thinking this whole episode to be more than a little surreal.

"More to the point. I am not simply some selfish old soul, who cannot be bothered with anybody. You really must understand something. Imagine how difficult it would be for them to embrace this new knowledge. All the while, since the time of their 'Enlightenment', they have been convinced that their ways of explaining how reality works can be attributed to rules, formulas and predictability. Now, can you imagine the crisis that this would put them in? The whole of their meanings as they know them would be thrown into disarray. I cannot do that to them. It is better that they be left to their illusions, until the day that these illusions shatter and break in front of them. At that point they will truly realise that some things are better left as stories. That way, they will retain a proper sense of their place within the scheme of things. This will be the best chance for the rest of us not to be placed in a zoo or a laboratory. Think on and keep my secret."

And so George, who was now getting quite low on air returned slowly to the surface.

As he broke through the water Fred said "By heck lad you gave us a bit of a fright there. All those bubbles for five minutes and no sign of you. What happened down there?"

"Well" said George, "I had to have a good scout around, obviously. I came to some vegetation and saw something moving behind it. But when I got there it was just many strands of seaweed flailing around like massive gangly arms. But alas, I must report that there was no Octopus there."

And with that Fred started darting around in a wild frenzy. "Told you so, Florence!"

"Calls himself a scientist!" Florence chortled. "Has he never heard of falsifiability?" she whispered to George, as Fred went berserk with feelings of triumph.

"Ey Fred," she shouted. "Just because Octopus was not here, doesn't mean he won't be found somewhere else."

And with that the two seagulls flew off, picking at each other about who was right and who was wrong. But George was the one who knew the truth and he realised that Octopus was correct. The people would argue and believe they were right. But some stories should not, in these times at any rate, be exposed to the light.

He too flew off now, in the direction of the White Cliffs of Dover, with both a secret to keep and a knowing smile on his face.

Chapter 3

Ode to Sabat

That seventh night, Sabat commanded the moon and stars "Shine!" But they refused, for he was lazy - "no work" his motto. "Sabat, climb a mountain", the darkness whispered back. So he summoned ten thousand forest ants to carry him. "Halt" they cried, upon reaching a ravine. All was not lost though, since Owl had seen. Riding her wings, progress was made, until elements roared "no!" and Owl's strength failed. Mountain goat roused from slumber and looking up, offered his strong back. Upon reaching the summit and looking around, sunrise unveiled day one's rebirth, whereupon smiling Sabat breathed his last.

Chapter 4

The Little Boy and the Distinguished Squirrel

They chased one another like kittens at play and smothered the night with crystalline perfection. But it was not a scientist's eye that watched them.

The latticed window separating the little boy from the snow hardly seemed there. The fragmented reflection peering back at him went unnoticed, as flakes of svelte whiteness captured his soul. The spell was broken only in that moment when darkness was turned incandescent by an eruption of lightning. Startled, Timothy took a step back. His memories flashed like the fire bolt, back to summer storms and humid classrooms where 'hot air meets cold' had displaced Leviathan myths of the gods' displeasure.

Lightning and snow in the Christmas break made him long for his schooling again. He turned and made for the table lamp to add some luminosity to the scene. As he reached for the pull cord however, another surge of brilliant blue light arrived from on high. The momentary hue showcased the painting on the wall. It was a simple depiction – a naked tree, atop a snow-covered hill. But Timothy, distracted, barely took it in. There had been no thunder. *No thunder?* Something courted the silence; tinged the air. Yet his flesh did not creep; for it was not eerie. A further ruptured vein of electricity cascaded around the sky. Then it came, shattering the stillness; CRACK! And suddenly, he was there. Not a window, not a room was in sight; just a tree at the crown of a hill.

Pins and needles greeted his feet as the icy snow chilled quickly through his training shoes. 'Better get moving' he thought, after surveying the scene. He trudged toward the ghostly form because there was nothing but snow from horizon to horizon. As he got closer to the tree he could see that it was bare, save for a single yellow leaf of modest size. Arriving under a bough he observed the outline of a door, set in the trunk. There was no handle but there was, at his eye line, a knocker. Timothy rattled it four times and waited. After a couple of minutes he repeated his knocks, only for the door to open soon after, with a voice muttering "yes, yes, yes. It takes a few moments to get here you know!"

Timothy was astonished to see a red squirrel, around half his own height, stood at the doorway. "Welcome to Weepy Willow, Master Timothy," it said, bidding him enter with a bow and a sweep of its forearm. "I am Rufus the Red, at your service."

Once Timothy had ventured inside, he replied "nice to meet you" and then gazed upward. 'Such a HUGE tree', he mused. There was a spiral staircase that reached up, seemingly without end. The light, which shone with a reassuring hint of pink, was provided solely by the stairs, which glowed serenely.

"Why am I here?" Timothy asked.
"Look outside the door a moment. What do you see in the snow?" Rufus responded.
"My footprints" Timothy confirmed.
"Well, that is how you got here!"
"No! Why did I get to be in *this* world?"
"Footprints, Timothy! Just as with my tail, one always leaves a trail."

Timothy scratched his head, sporting a puzzled frown.
"Anyhow, why is there only one leaf on this tree of yours?"
"So many questions young fellow, all to be answered in time. Perhaps first you would like a hot drink, to warm you up?"
"Yes please!" came the eager reply. *What a friendly squirrel* the little boy thought.
Rufus turned and hopped onto the first step. "Come on then!"

As the pair began their climb, Timothy could see large, framed photographs. They seemed to climb with them in a spiral around the tree walls. All of them were black and white and each looked somewhat distorted, as if set in a carnival's Hall of Mirrors.

"Why are these pictures black and white and bendy, Rufus?" Timothy queried.

"Well, it is because they absorb colour, Master Tim."

'Tim?' the little boy mused, 'sounds very grown up to me'. Nobody else called him that.

He was intrigued by the pictures. Though distorted he could make out that one was of a huge aeroplane with lines of smoke in tow and the next was of a child squatting in a vast rubbish dump. Yet another captured three tall chimneys belching smoke into the air. Then there was a television with a remote control.

'How odd' Timothy thought, all the while pondering how long it would be until the climb would be over and he would be enjoying his warming drink.

The last picture Timothy looked at was of a man in a forest with a chainsaw, cutting down a tree. "Nearly there" Rufus exclaimed, as if reading the youngster's recent thoughts. But now Timothy's mind was on something else.

Plink, plink, plink, came the faint echo, as if they were nearing a well.

"Did you say this is Weepy Willow, Rufus?"

"Yes"

"But trees do not cry. Surely it isn't the sound of tears I can hear now?"

"Master Tim, anything is possible in the imagination. It weaves worlds together – worlds within worlds. But yes, the tree is sad for all the things that will one day come to pass in the natural world."

Meanwhile, the pair had reached a platform that led to a door, even though the tree continued upward. Opening it and passing through, the pair stood in a modestly fitted room.

"Okay, let me now make you that drink I promised. What would you like?"

"What do you have?"

"Nettle tea"

"Nettle tea! Is that it?"

"Young man, there are no supermarkets around here! Even if there were one beyond the horizon, I have no car to transport me. And I am a squirrel, in case you hadn't noticed. So I harvested and stored the nettles before the snow came. Besides, nettle tea is good for you."

"Alright, I'll have some" Timothy said, unsure of what he was letting himself in for.

Rufus went over to the tap and measured two mugs of water, which he placed into a pan, before taking his spoon and adding the leaves. Next, he switched his cooker on and turned a dial. The hob lit up with the same pink tinge as the staircase.

"Wow!" Timothy exclaimed, "I *love* that pink. It looks nothing like the cooker rings at home or in my friends' houses. Where did you get it?"

"This tree has a lovely friendship with the Sun and all our energy comes naturally from our kindly star," Rufus replied. "Pure energy, untouched by humans, glows in pretty pink."

After the nettle infusion was prepared, Rufus retrieved his tea strainer, before pouring them each a steaming mug. He scampered to his rocking chair, sat down, and invited Timothy to do likewise. The little boy looked intently at the talking squirrel in front of him and asked "Is this real?"

"Of course," came the reply.

"So I didn't imagine my footprints?"

"Because something is in your imagination that doesn't mean it isn't real, Master Tim. Many real things start in the imagination."

"But the single leaf on this tree wasn't on the painting in my own house. Is *that* real?"

"It is indeed. But it is more than a leaf. The leaf is you."

"Me?"

"Yes you. A little boy who most people don't notice, just like they don't notice their footprints, because they aren't looking or even thinking."

"But all this can't be real, because people don't live in a world like this one," Timothy said.

"But people *do* live in worlds like the pictures you saw as we climbed and although you are growing up in the nineteen seventies, the world will become increasingly drained of its colour and beauty. That *will* be real."

"Why will things get like that, Rufus?"

"Young man, before the Industrial Revolution, when there were but few folk upon the earth and before large cities grew, humans could afford not to think much about how they lived their lives and created waste and used the good things of the land. But the earth she is becoming exhausted as numbers increase, because most live without thought and do not see."

Timothy sipped his nettle tea. It tasted odd. The whole situation was odd but, strangely, what Rufus was saying didn't feel odd.

"But what can *I* do?"

"You can dream dreams and so keep your heart and intentions noble."

"Is that all?" Timothy asked.

"No, that is not all. You must use your imagination but act as well. You must help others to picture a different world."

"How can I do that, Rufus?"

49

"The first thing you must always do, Master Tim, is conserve. You saw me make the tea. I always measure out enough for what is needed – never more. Do likewise. This is a simple message you can pass on to others."

Timothy and Rufus spent a few moments in silence; Rufus rocking in his chair and Timothy wondering what his friends would make of all this.

"Can I still have fun?" Timothy blurted out.
"Of course, young man. It is important that you do."

The squirrel looked down at his watch and said "It has been lovely to meet up with you, young Tim. And now it is time for you to return home. I myself am due another visitor soon; a little girl called Agnes, I believe."

Timothy rose from his chair and Rufus did likewise. Soon, they were making their way back down the spiral staircase. As they were nearing the bottom, Timothy realised that he must ask one last question of his hospitable friend.
"You said the leaf on the tree is me?"
"Yes"
"Well, how come it is yellow?"
"I'm glad you asked me that Master Tim. I knew that you would!"

As they reached the ground, Rufus offered a box to the boy. Opening it he could see that it was a palette of many vivid colours of paint. "There are no brushes Timothy because this is magic paint and you can paint with your mind. The black and white photographs you have seen, suck colour from the world - you can draw it back by bringing your imagination and action into everything you touch in the world."

"Really? But you have not answered my question about the yellow leaf."

"The leaf teeters between green and brown, life and death. It is yellow now because its life is ebbing away but you can help bring it back. While there is you, there is hope."

"But what will happen to the magic when I grow up, Rufus?"

"Master Tim, try not to worry. Everything changes."

"Everything?" Tim repeated.

"Everything and much is lost besides. Indeed, one day I will be replaced by someone who is grey – but not because I will be old."

Timothy did not understand these words but smiled at his furry mentor as he said "thank you for everything, Rufus."

Rufus smiled back and extended his furry paw toward the boy, who reached out his hand to clasp it.

No more words were shared but "goodbye Timothy" followed by "goodbye Rufus".

Holding his box of paints close to his chest, Timothy set off in the direction from which he had come, down the hill. He followed the original set of prints he had left in the snow. Turning around after a minute he waved to Rufus, who waved back. After another thirty seconds he turned and waved once more. Only this time, Rufus had gone.

'Ho hum, what now?' Timothy mused, as he looked around with his thoughts turning to home. He was feeling quite at a loss about his next move. So the sound of a 'CRACK!' accompanied by a 'whoosh' were almost a relief, as Timothy experienced a feeling of dropping through a chute of snow. In an instant he was again facing the picture of the tree on the snow-covered hill.

The lightning lit it up and he noticed that it was different. There was now a single yellow leaf that had not been there before. His shoes felt a little damp as well. 'Did that really happen?' Timothy pondered. 'Okay, imagination at the ready'. He concentrated as hard as he could on making the leaf green. But, try as he might, each fresh blue lightning bolt illuminated a tree with a still yellow leaf. Undeterred, Timothy turned and walked back over to the latticed window and focused hard on what he wished for.

Half a minute later a zig zag erupted and a bolt of pink lightning lit up the sky. "Awesome, Rufus!" Timothy shrieked out excitedly. And then he heard it. 'Plink, plink, plink'. 'What's happening?' He could tell the noise was nearby. Investigating, he moved out into the hallway. All the while, the noise got louder. When he finally reached the downstairs WC, Timothy realised a tap was dripping. Without further ado he tightened it and the plinks ceased.

Timothy crept back into the study and switched on the table lamp. He looked up and saw that the tree's solitary leaf seemed a little greener than before. 'Was this a trick of the light?' he wondered. Excited by everything, he resolved to wake up his dad and tell him everything. He switched the lamp off and left the study.

After he made his way upstairs, Timothy saw his father's half-open bedroom door. Light was streaming out; illuminating the landing. Timothy popped inside the room to find his father snoring. A heater was on at full power near the bed. Timothy saw a remote control lying on the duvet and a small red light shining on the TV.

"Dad, dad, I had a strange dream" the boy said loudly. Timothy's dad roused, startled.

"Go to bed son, it's late" he said, turning onto his side.

"But dad, I met a talking squirrel and he told me lots of things about saving energy."

Timothy's dad sat up and rubbed his eyes, thinking that he should make some effort, or he would never coax Timothy to turn in.

"What did he say, son?"

Timothy walked over to the TV and pressed the off button. "This will save energy", he said. "Rufus said we need to do that."

"Rufus?"

"Yes, Rufus" he confirmed. "And you have a light on and a heater on full with your door open, dad."

Timothy's father wondered at just who was responsible for the school curriculum nowadays. But he couldn't find fault with his son's logic. "Okay, I'll turn my heater down and my light off when you go. Close the door behind you when you leave."

"The Weepy Willow will be happy now, dad."

"Okay son, now go and get some sleep. You'll be helping me clear snow in the morning."

Timothy left with a smile as his father turned off the light. He closed the bedroom door behind him.

After he got to his room and curled up in his bed, many things floated through his imagination about that day. He soon drifted off into a satisfying sleep. In the land of dreams Timothy could not see the picture in the study that now sported two leaves – one bright green and the other light yellow.

But Rufus could.

Chapter 5

The Endless Dying of the Light

Rosie's toes were frozen: Just like her heart. The sock puppet her tiny fist had clenched, soon landed in the snow. Its mouth told no stories, but its eyes had seen a few, just like Rosie's. Propped against a lamp post, its eyes stared across the street into the pawn shop window, as if mesmerised watching a cinematic epic. A young mother remonstrated "just five more for Christmas dinner, PLEASE!" "Sorry ma'am" came the reply. Meanwhile torrential rain had become a flood. And so another story, along with Rosie's, was washed away with the puppet. I was that puppet once.

Chapter 6

The Tiny Spider and the Gargantuan Fly

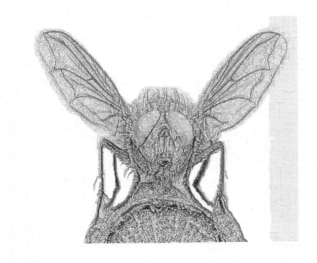

"Come on Edward", the boy's mother shouted up from downstairs. "At this rate, we are going to be late for school again."

Edward was twelve years old and had recently started at secondary school. It had felt different somehow. When he had been in primary school everything within his experience unfurled as if life were fun, time were slow and nobody in authority was interested in bending you into shape. Today he dreamed of the lunch break and any opportunity to chat up Elizabeth.

"Yes mum," Edward shouted down. "Just a few minutes more while I straighten my tie and polish my shoes." Edward had already done these things but he wanted a few more minutes breathing space to compose himself.

He looked in the mirror. He could see pimples. He was only pleased it was not acne. It really did not impress him how his father always got the local barber to do a basic 'basin' cut of his hair. It looked horrendous and all his classmates ribbed him for it. Oh and those dreadful, cheap National Health Service spectacles (his parents had known more than their share of poverty). He always used to take them off after his mum dropped him off near the school in the car, for fear of mockery. But then he would have to run fast to every class between rooms, just to secure the front seat, because he just could not see the blackboard from farther away. The other children did not understand of course (how could they?) that this was not a choice. Their constant teasing "teacher's pet, teacher's pet", was hard to handle – especially when a deeper truth was being hidden – one too painful to make public.

Looking more intently than ever before he did not, at first, notice the gargantuan fly which had made its way into his room through the open window. It had recently landed and was now crawling from the base of the mirror, slowly up toward his eye line. He was in truth too busy loathing himself.

But when he did see it he had such a fright and recoiled instantly. The fly seemed unperturbed. It appeared to be absorbed with preening itself. Working over its legs, sides and wings in a systematic fashion. He moved closer to inspect the creature more closely. "So gross" he muttered under his breath.

"So gross? How cheeky are you?" a buzzing voice said.

The young man jumped back. Was this his own mind in convincing voice, trying to trick him into believing a fly had just spoken to him? He pondered that for a moment, then moved close in again. "Well you are!

Everybody knows that flies are dirty and carry disease."

"They taught you well at school I see, young man."

"It IS true!"

"Did you not just see me cleaning myself all over? I was using this mirror to make sure that no part of the process was missed out. Anyway, look at you! You don't see me looking at my reflection and deciding to beat myself up about all my little imperfections, do you?"

This was an ouch moment for the boy, who had failed to realise just how absorbed he had become in being down on himself, until this rather large fly had interrupted him.

"Edward hurry up!" his mother shouted, with much more impatience this time.

"Coming mum." Edward yelled back. But he said nothing more to the fly. He simply picked up his old tatty satchel full of homework, fled his room and hoped this unwelcome guest would have flown back out of the window and away, by the time of his return from his educational captivity.

The trip in the car exhibited its usual features.

"So remember, tell Ms Smith that you need extra help with art. And don't forget to attend the chess club meeting at lunch. Make sure you keep your uniform tidy throughout the day."

"Yes mum" Edward mumbled on autopilot.

As they arrived she said "Give your mum a kiss."

Edward leaned over and kissed his mother on the cheek. Unfortunately for him, some teenagers had seen this and took the opportunity later on to rib him about it relentlessly. He really wondered whether, when the old religious teachers at Sunday School were talking about the punishments of hell, they really had schooldays in mind. At lunch break he was handed no respite, since it turned out that Elizabeth (his secret crush) was off sick today. He was gutted when he found this out and decided to take his packed lunch into an area at the school perimeter that was enclosed by bushes. In that place he could hope to avoid the usual unwanted attention of his taunting adversaries.

As he sat there in the Sun, hidden and enjoying his sandwiches now that he was in peace, he started to think bad thoughts about these people who constantly made sport of him. He then heard his mother's voice and the voice of his Sunday School teachers in his head "You mustn't think bad thoughts." Edward tried his hardest to follow these words now. But the more he tried to do it, the worse the thoughts became. He started to brood. He thought it perhaps high time that these infidels be taught a lesson, for their constant warring against him. What had he done? What had he EVER done? Apart that was, from being criticised, nagged and otherwise instructed on what to do and how to be and even WHO to be.

'Anger is bad' another voice inside his head then said to him.

"No it is not" came the reply from one of the bushes nearby. Seemingly this was going to be one of those days. First talking insects, now talking plants? More disturbing, he realised, was how it could seemingly hear what was going on *inside his head*. He walked over to the bush, but could see nothing unusual.

"Are you a talking bush? Today I have already had a conversation with a fly."

"I am no bush" the voice retorted. "Look more closely."
As he did so, the boy could see a delicate cobweb lattice, at the centre of which was a spider that was just a few millimetres in diameter.

"Everyone I know says you should not entertain bad thoughts, so how can a tiny spider like you know better than all of them?"

"Because I sit here patiently" said the diminutive arachnid. "I watch things come and I watch things go and I see the things which remain and also the things which perish. And then I wait some more and in the end, all the things I need *come to me*."

"And what has *that* got to do with thinking bad thoughts or being angry?" the young boy retorted.

"Plenty! You know that feelings come and feelings go, right?"

"Yes."

"Well then, why would you hold onto feelings and thoughts, as if they were any kind of reliable guide to the truth about anything? And why would you either silence your persistent feelings or just express them, rather than allowing them just to be what they are."

"And what are they then?"

"Things which pass" the spider replied. "So denying what others' treatment of you makes you feel, or instead wanting to harm them, is just coming from a hidden place."

"And where is that?"

"The place that the gargantuan fly told you about this morning."

"What? How do you know him?"

"We are all connected, young man."

"So if that is true, why do spiders eat flies?"

"There is a natural order of things, Edward."

Edward was a little unsettled that the tiny spider knew his name. "How do you know my name? And what exactly is natural about eating those you are acquainted with?"

"All in good time, young man." And with that the tiny spider scuttled away into the bushes, leaving Edward alone with his thoughts and feelings.

Later on in the geography lesson, Edward had been rebuked for not paying attention. He was near the back of the class and could not see the blackboard. When confronted by the teacher about his inattention, he had to mention his short-sightedness and subsequently to endure the humiliation of putting on the cheap spectacles he had in his blazer pocket. When the teacher left the room for a few minutes to retrieve some props, Edward was treated to his usual jibes of 'pizza face', now added to with the standard 'four eyes' taunts. His rage was close to spilling over now. But he remembered the words of Spider, just in time. He wondered for just how long he would have to face these kinds of trial in his life. Cruelty was something he vowed never to inflict upon any other living soul, from those moments on. Maybe Spider knew better than all those other human voices after all.

At the end of a long day, the final bell rang at 3.15pm. Edward raced out of the school and breathed a huge sigh of relief, once he got into his mother's car.

"Did you do all those things I told you? Look, your blazer has a green mark on it. It looks like you have been lying in long grass playing hide and seek or something. What do I have to do to drum these lessons in, young man?"

At this point Edward did not really care about what his mother was complaining about. He just wanted to let this pass too, get home and chat further with the intriguing gargantuan fly.

When he got into his room he threw down his satchel onto his bed and started to scan the room meticulously. He could not see anything and neither could he hear any buzzing noise. The window was now shut. His mother must have closed it during the day. He wondered if this teacher of his might return at some point, because he had questions to ask.

"Fly, Fly" he called out.

But then he heard a different voice – not the buzzing one he remembered Fly having. It whispered "Here Edward, here."

Locating the voice, his eyes peered up to the ceiling and one of the corners of his room. There was a spider in its web. "I am the cousin of the little one you spoke with earlier at the bush. I see that you have already put some of her lessons into practice with your schoolmates."

"Yes, but I am sick of the constant struggle and having to overcome one obstacle after the other."

"Remember the lesson that Fly taught you this morning. It is important for you not to take these struggles and make them the thing which you feel defines you. You made progress today when you were patient in the face of trials."

"And where is Fly? He was here this morning but seems to have flown away."

With this Spider said "look into my web."

There in the middle of it was a large bundle of cobweb silk wrapped around an object that was large in size. "There is Fly" said Spider. "Inside my wrapping and ready to be a tasty meal later."

"But your cousin said everything is related. And when I asked why spiders eat flies he said it is the natural order of things."

"Yes, it is" the larger arachnid replied. "But for you there are lessons to be understood in all that unfolds in these natural ways."

"I liked Fly" Edward protested.

"No you didn't! You told him he was dirty."

"But when I looked further it was possible to see that this thing I'd been taught at school was not really true."

"So" said Spider "can you see what should be most natural for *you*?"

"I have no idea what you mean, Spider" the boy replied.

"Fly helps you overcome external obstacles and gives you the perseverance to survive all the challenges that will appear all around you. He teaches self-acceptance. He is male that is just what he does. We spiders are female. We do not care about that. And that is because when you have true mastery nothing outside you matters. The internal obstacles of self are the ones you must truly overcome. Once you do, it is natural that your inner strength will consume everything which Fly ever gave you temporary strength to overcome. Once you achieve inner composure, everything shall be possible for you and the old struggles shall be consumed, just like Fly.

This is the natural order of things and is the truth about why Spider will always eat Fly."

And with that, Edward relaxed. He understood that he'd been given an equally precious gift by both Spider and Fly. He went downstairs and smiled. Entering the kitchen where his mother was preparing their evening meal, he said "I love you mum. I'm really looking forward to something tasty to eat."

Chapter 7

The Nightingale and the Owl

The forest council meeting had come to order at its appointed time of noon. Unfortunately for Nuala, Owl could not be present because he was on a business trip. So instead, it had been left to Squirrel to preside over the affairs of the day.

"First item on the agenda this day" Squirrel stated formally "is the matter of Nuala the Nightingale singing at night and disturbing all the other forest residents. How plead you, madam?"

"Unlike most of you, I have no partner" said Nuala, "with whom to share what is in my heart. It is heavy all of the time. Please, my singing is only to find someone to love and cherish and who will love and cherish me in return."

The creatures took some time to discuss this matter with each other and after they had done so for several minutes, Badger approached Squirrel and whispered in his ear. A few minutes later Squirrel addressed the gathering. "It has been established that Nuala's singing at unsocial hours has disturbed the lives of our citizens too much. So the decree I must issue is that of banishment for the sake of the rest of our community. Miss Nightingale, you may return home to make preparations for departure, but must leave this place by nightfall."

Nuala was distraught. She returned to her forest abode and sat there for just a few minutes, wondering what to do and where to go. 'I shall travel far from this unwelcoming place' she thought to herself, before her upset escalated, prompting her to flee quickly with a tear in her eye. She set off at speed and flew and flew and flew. Eventually she arrived at a large oak tree and immediately nestled between its branches into the cover, so she could hide and console herself. The only thing she could do after soothing her aching heart was sing. It was her only remaining pleasure. After many a day and night in her melancholy state, instead of singing through the night she fell asleep and dreamed a dream. All she could really remember upon waking was a repeating 'cuckoo' sound. Nuala opened her beak wide to begin her song once again. Only, on this still dark morning, there was nothing. Her singing voice had disappeared. She tried again... and again, but to no avail. Feeling this to be too much to bear, the weary nightingale began to lament and weep with an outpouring of tears that had perhaps *never* been known.

Just before the Sun was due to rise, Owl passed by on his return journey from visiting an old friend. He heard sobbing in the old oak tree and stopped to investigate. Perching next to Nuala he said "I heard that you had been exiled. But nobody could tell me where you had gone."

"Oh Owl, Owl my sweet friend. I just had to escape and be on my own. It has been awful from the first minute of the forest meeting until now. And, just last night, something happened to make things much worse. I woke to find even my singing voice taken from me."

"What happened?"

"I remember nothing, other than dreaming the whole night. Yet what I can recall is only the repeated cry 'cuckoo', 'cuckoo', 'cuckoo'."

"Oh Nuala, cuckoos are thieves. Legend implicates them in the stealing of beautiful voices for bounty, in order to take them to the mountains, where they echo forever to entertain the giants."

"Then I am completely lost, Owl."

"Fear not" he replied, "for I believe that I know the whereabouts of these mountains and that we can set out in high hopes of retrieving your voice."

Nevertheless, although the Sun had now risen, thick dark clouds had completely obscured it in the sky. It

would prove hard to navigate with such dim conditions. It had also now become icy cold; so cold in fact that Nuala imagined that it might freeze her blood and glue her wings to her body.
Serendipitously, at that very moment a beautiful and large, vibrant butterfly appeared, which was so bright that it compensated for the blocking of the Sun. Nuala's hopes rose momentarily. But then she said "how shall I fly in this cold?"

But Owl reassured, "Flap your wings vigorously for 15 minutes and that will warm you up and stop your wings from sticking to your body." Just then a ferocious gale whipped up. Nuala was unsure how much more she could take. Even if she followed Owl's instructions the butterfly would be severely buffeted. But Owl was wise and knew her thoughts. He said "Let Butterfly and I come with you on your way and my wings shall shield you both from the gale. Once we reach the enchanted forest it will help provide protection, until we reach the mountains where the giants live."

And so it was that the trio set off with warmth, light and shelter, despite the raging conditions. Even though the surroundings were so inhospitable, it still proved possible for the three of them to make it into the enchanted forest in under one hour. Things became considerably easier then. After only one more hour of travelling through the forest, Nuala could finally see looming mountains above the forest canopy, toward the horizon. She felt a small pang of hope now, as they made good progress.

Around fifty minutes later, the three of them arrived at the base of the mountains and began their ascent. It took them a while flying and the increase of altitude proved a challenge. But eventually they made it to a plateau and then headed into the extensive mountain range. After a relatively brief descent they found themselves in a valley, with a river flowing through the middle of it. Owl made a hooting sound and its echoes reverberated all around.

"Okay, now what do we do, Owl?"

"I will fly around here and try to locate where the giants may be, in order to begin our plan to retrieve your singing voice." And soon he was away. After half an hour there was no sign of Owl. This was upsetting to Nuala and she had no idea what to do next. Was this story about giants and echoes and cuckoo thieves going to be proven untrue? Certainly, Owl's voice had echoed beautifully, so she thought maybe the story did have merit. Ten minutes later and still with no sign of Owl, Nuala asked Butterfly to go check where he may be and perhaps fetch him back. She was somewhat unnerved after Butterfly flew off. For there was no dimming of the light. The Sun was shining once more.

As Nuala gazed longingly at the beautiful lush trees all around her as well as the grass and the water, full of vitality, she began to experience a delicious feeling welling up from deep inside her. She opened her beak and began to sing. Within seconds the beautiful echo of her own voice began to resound all around the rocks in the valley. 'Ah! This must be exactly why the mountain giants so desired to capture sweet voices' she thought to herself. Once again, heart full of joy, she began to sing out her finest tune. She stopped and then again for several seconds, her voice reverberated deliciously around this idyllic canyon.

'One more time', she thought to herself. And so she broke into the most beautiful melody once more and then stopped. The music again reflected back to her and she felt such joy. But then she noticed that the beautiful singing was continuing to echo. It did not stop. But then, a few moments later, it did stop. Only a few seconds later again, it started afresh. She was at first a little worried that this may signal the giants being nearby. This time though it was coming not from the rocks but from a nearby tree. Curious, she flew over and landed in the branches of what was a beautiful oak. She was amazed to discover that it was another bird. "Who are you?" she asked.

"My name is Nathaniel" came the reply. "I am a nightingale who lost his voice. Who then are you?"

Owl and Butterfly never did return. In fact Nuala began to wonder if Owl had planned that very eventuality all along. Yet now it did not seem to matter quite so much. As evening fell, and with no giants anywhere in sight, Nuala and Nathaniel together sang the most beautiful duet ever heard – all night long.

44701100R00049

Printed in Poland
by Amazon Fulfillment
Poland Sp. z o.o., Wrocław